Out Of Control

by Steven Butler
Illustrated by Bill Ledger

Houghton Mifflin Harcourt.

In this story ...

Jin
(Swoop)

Jin has the power to fly. He once had a race with a jumbo jet ... and won! He can fly high enough to reach outer space!

Evan
(Flex)

Cam
(Switch)

Nisha
(Nimbus)

Mr. Trainer
(teacher)

"Watch me, Mr. Trainer!" shouted Jin.

Jin spun into his superhero costume and became Swoop. The class was doing P.E. (Power Exploration), and Swoop wanted to show off his skills.

"OK, Swoop," said Mr. Trainer. "Let's see what you can do!"

"Stand back, everyone," Swoop said excitedly.

Swoop shot into the sky like a rocket.

"Wheeeeeeee!" he shouted, as he looped around a cloud in a huge circle.

Swoop wanted to be at the top of the class this week. The student with the highest grades was going to receive a Hero Academy gold merit badge.

Swoop grinned to himself. He could already imagine the gold merit badge pinned on his uniform.

Swoop whizzed around the sports field, and zoomed through the holo-hoops and under the power-poles. He landed right in front of his classmates.

"Wow!" Flex yelled.

"That was terrific!" shouted Switch.

Swoop felt like he might burst with pride. Surely he'd win the gold merit badge?

"Great job," said Mr. Trainer. "Now, who's next?"

"Me! Me! Me!" everyone shouted.

Swoop watched his friends show off their super-skills. Switch turned into a cheetah and sprinted around the school.

Then Nimbus conjured up a snow storm.

Swoop was starting to feel less and less confident that he would win the gold merit badge. His friends' super-skills were terrific. He had to do something more amazing if he wanted to be at the top of the class.

Swoop marched in front of the group.

"I've got something else to show you," he said. "I'm going to fly higher than any hero has ever flown before."

Mr. Trainer frowned. "Hang on, Swoop," he said. "You've had your turn."

Before Mr. Trainer could stop him, Swoop was soaring into the air. He went higher and higher, until he started to feel dizzy.

Swoop took a deep breath and closed his eyes tightly. He didn't like to admit it, but he had always been a bit scared of heights.

"Just keep going," he whispered to himself. "Think of the gold merit badge."

Swoop opened one eye. Beneath him, Hero Academy was getting smaller and smaller.

"I'm sure to win now," he thought.

Swoop rocketed up, until Lexis City was
far below.

"Just a little further," he said to himself.

Swoop flew up through the clouds. He could
feel the air around him getting icy cold.

He could see darkness above him, and the curve of the Earth below.

Swoop gasped. He was almost in space!

Swoop tried to slow down, but he couldn't....
He was flying too fast! He started to panic.

"HELP!" Swoop cried.

Just then, he heard a humming sound. As it got closer, he realized it was the rumble of an engine.

It was the Hero Academy jet!
The jet was used when the heroes needed
to go on long-distance missions.

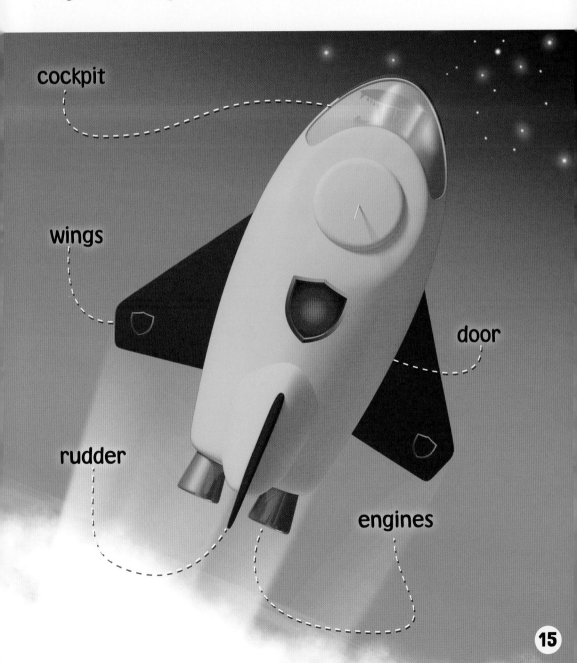

cockpit

wings

door

rudder

engines

The hatch of the plane opened and Mr. Trainer leaned out.

"Swoop!" he shouted, over the rushing wind. "What on earth do you think you are doing?"

"I can't stop!" Swoop shouted back.

Mr. Trainer slammed the hatch shut. A second later, the door opened. "Don't panic, Swoop," a voice yelled. It was Flex. "I still haven't shown my power today."

Flex held onto the plane door with one hand and stretched out toward Swoop.

"Please hurry!" Swoop shouted. He was getting farther and farther away from the jet. In only a few more moments, he'd be lost in outer space forever.

"Got you!" Flex grabbed Swoop by the ankle and yanked him back toward the jet.

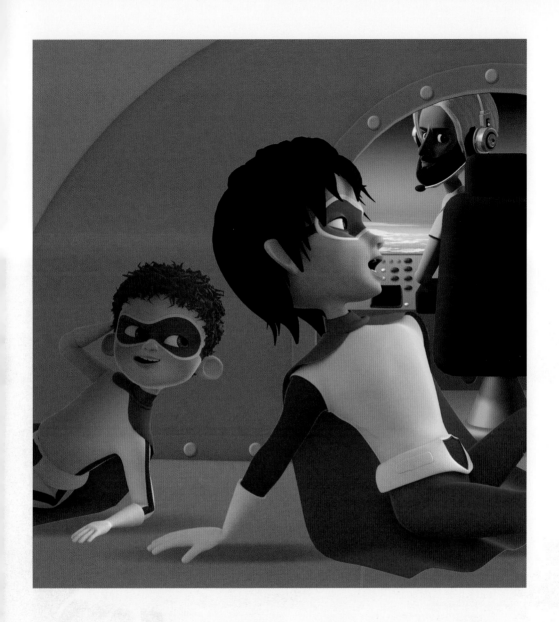

The two boys tumbled in through the open door and landed on the floor of the cabin.

Mr. Trainer looked at Swoop crossly.

"Ummm ... sorry," Swoop said.

Mr. Trainer raised one eyebrow. "Swoop," he said. "I'm glad you're safe, but what you did was extremely dangerous. You have a no-flying detention for a week."

"Yes, Mr. Trainer," said Swoop. He looked down at his feet. They'd be staying firmly on the ground for a while.

Swoop sat in silence for the rest of the journey back to Hero Academy. His heart was still pounding and his hands wouldn't stop shaking.

When the jet landed at the sports field, Switch and Nimbus rushed to meet it.

"I just wanted to win the gold merit badge," Swoop said.

"Are you sure you're all right?" Nimbus asked.

"I'm fine," mumbled Swoop. "Except for nearly getting lost in space!"

"Cheer up, Swoop," Flex said. "It's not so bad."

"What do you mean?" asked Swoop.

"Mr. Trainer just told me you broke the school record for the highest ever flight," Flex replied.

Swoop whooped.

Flex blushed. "And *I* broke the school record for the highest hero rescue ever!"

"Well done," Mr. Trainer said, as he handed Flex the gold merit badge.

Swoop grinned at his friend. "You really deserve to win," he added.

"Maybe you'll get the badge next time," Flex replied.

"Maybe," said Swoop. "But I'll be practicing my flying skills closer to the ground from now on!"